Money Count$

Lisa Zamosky

MONEY COUNTS

Characters

Narrator 1   Melissa

Ben   Mr. Cash

Narrator 2   Mrs. Cash

Setting

This reader's theater takes place in and around the home of Mr. and Mrs. Cash.

Mr. Cash

Mrs. Cash

Ben

Melissa

Act 1

Narrator 1:   A man and woman just moved into the house next door to Ben and Melissa.

Ben: "Melissa, look at the sign in our neighbor's yard."

Narrator 2:   The sign says, "Help Wanted."

Melissa: "Ben, this could be our chance to make some money!"

Ben: "Let's see what we have to do."

Narrator 1:	Ben and Melissa walk to their neighbor's house. They see a bunch of other signs in the yard.
Melissa:	"Look at this sign, Ben. It says we could make one dollar if we sweep the front porch."
Narrator 2:	Just then, Melissa and Ben hear voices.
Mr. Cash:	"Hello! I'm Mr. Cash and this is my wife, Mrs. Cash. We're your new neighbors."
Melissa:	"Hi! I'm Melissa and this is my brother, Ben."
Ben:	"We saw the sign in your front yard, Mr. Cash. It says you need help around the house."
Mr. Cash:	"That's right, Ben. This old house needs a lot of work. We would gladly pay anyone who's willing to help."
Melissa:	"I'll sweep your front porch. The sign says you'll pay one dollar for that job."
Narrator 1:	Melissa sweeps the porch quickly. She's very pleased with her work.

Mrs. Cash: "Melissa, you have earned one dollar. How would you like to be paid?"

Melissa: "What do you mean?"

Mr. Cash: "We could pay you with a dollar bill. Or, maybe you'd like four quarters instead?"

Melissa: "Does it matter?"

Mrs. Cash: "Nope. It's all the same amount of money."

Melissa: "Then, I'll take the four quarters."

Ben: "I'll rake the leaves in your front yard. The sign says that job pays five dollars."

Mrs. Cash: "That's right, Ben. For your hard work, you'll be five dollars richer! We could pay you with a five-dollar bill or five one-dollar bills. Either way, it's still five dollars."

Narrator 2: Ben and Melissa begin to daydream about how they'll spend their money.

Mrs. Cash:	"Melissa, one piece of bubblegum costs twenty-five cents. You could buy four pieces with one dollar."
Mr. Cash:	"A marble costs one cent. You could buy one hundred marbles with one dollar."
Ben:	"What about me? What could I buy with five dollars?"
Melissa:	"You could buy ten cookies, if they cost fifty cents each."
Ben:	"Or, I could buy five packets of baseball cards. They're only one dollar each."
Mrs. Cash:	"When you have money, you need to decide if you want to spend it or save it."
Mr. Cash:	"Saving money is important. You shouldn't always spend the money you get."
Mrs. Cash:	"Right! If you save your money, it will grow and grow."
Ben:	"Yeah! My dad says money grows on trees."

Melissa:	"No, Ben. You've got it all wrong. Dad is always telling you that money does NOT grow on trees."
Ben:	"Oh. Well, I wish it did. That would be so cool!"
Mrs. Cash:	"Of course money doesn't grow on trees. But if you save it rather than spend it right away, it will grow over time."
Mr. Cash:	"That's right! You could save your money at home in a piggy bank. Or, you could take your money to a real bank."
Mrs. Cash:	"If you want to save your money at the bank, you have to open a savings account. The account has your name on it so the bank knows it's your money."

Poem: Watching Money Grow

Act 2

Narrator 1:	Ben looks at another sign in the front yard. It says Mr. and Mrs. Cash will pay ten dollars to anyone who will cut the grass.
Narrator 2:	Ben cuts the grass in a flash.

Mr. Cash: "Terrific work, Ben! You've earned ten dollars. Would you like a ten-dollar bill or two five-dollar bills?"

Narrator 2: Ben doesn't answer. He's too busy thinking about how to spend his money.

Ben: "I could buy my mom some flowers for her birthday. I saw some roses at the flower shop for only fifty cents each. At that price, I could buy twenty roses with ten dollars."

Mrs. Cash:	"We could also give you ten dollars in coins. Would you like a stack of two hundred nickels?"
Narrator 1:	Ben stops to think for a moment. He isn't sure how he wants to be paid for his work.
Melissa:	"Remember, you could save your money instead."
Mr. Cash:	"Right. Once you open a savings account, you can add money to it whenever you want."
Mrs. Cash:	"The money you add to your account is called a deposit."
Mr. Cash:	"Even though you leave your money at the bank, it's still your money."
Mrs. Cash:	"After you've saved for awhile, you might want to buy something special."
Melissa:	"A bike!"
Ben:	"A video game!"
Mr. Cash:	"A new car!"

Mrs. Cash:	"Diamond earrings!"
Mr. Cash:	"Okay, let's not get carried away."
Mrs. Cash:	"So, when you want to take your money out of the bank, you make a withdrawal."
Mr. Cash:	"That's right. A withdrawal is how you get your money back from the bank."

Act 3

Narrator 1:	Melissa looks at the other signs in the yard. There is still a lot of work to be done. She decides to plant flowers and pull weeds.
Ben:	"Mrs. Cash, I think you should pay my sister one hundred dollars for her hard work,"
Narrator 2:	Ben says with a big smile.
Mrs. Cash:	"Okay, but we'll have to pay her with pennies."
Mr. Cash:	"That would be ten thousand pennies. Imagine that!"
Melissa:	"I'd need really big pockets to hold that many pennies."

Ben:	"What if I want to buy a house? I saw one up the street for sale. I think it costs one hundred thousand dollars!"
Melissa:	"We don't have that much money!"
Mrs. Cash:	"Not many people do."

Mr. Cash: "Most people borrow money from the bank to buy a house."

Melissa: "Would we have to pay back the money we borrowed?"

Mrs. Cash: "Yes, you would have to pay the bank a little each month for many, many years."

Act 4

Melissa: "What could we do to make one million dollars?"

Narrator 2: Mr. and Mrs. Cash look at each other and smile. They know just the job for Ben and Melissa.

Mr. Cash: "We have a job that will pay you one million dollars. You must be willing to work hard."

Ben and Melissa: "What is it?"

Mr. Cash: "You need to be good kids."

Mrs. Cash: "And you need to try hard in school."

Narrator 2: Ben and Melissa look at each other and say,

Ben and Melissa: "We can do that!"

Mr. and Mrs. Cash: "Great! Then, you may earn one million dollars during your lifetime,"

Narrator 1: Mr. and Mrs. Cash say with a wink.

Mr. Cash: "Do you know that a million dollars in quarters would weigh as much as a whale?"

Ben: "What if I had that much money in one-dollar bills?"

Mrs. Cash: "One million dollars in one-dollar bills would stand about three hundred sixty feet high!"

Melissa: "Whoa! That's one hundred and eleven meters. That IS a lot of money!"

Narrator 2: Mr. Cash, Mrs. Cash, Ben, and Melissa talk about all the things they would buy if they *really* had a million dollars.

Mr. Cash: "But, don't forget! You should also save some of your money."

**Ben and
Melissa:** "Wow! There are a lot of choices to make when you have money."

 Song: Money Counts Rap

WATCHING MONEY GROW

Saving money is what interests me,
Like money growing on a tree.
Deposit some and then you'll see
Your money grows and grows.

Saving money is saving me
From losing money rapidly.
Instead, I'm saving steadily
And my money grows and grows.

A wealth of wealth is right for me.
I'll save my money faithfully
And be as patient as can be
While my money grows and grows.

♫♪ MONEY COUNTS RAP ♫♪

Chorus
One, two, three, four, five
Money counts and that's no jive!
One, two, three, four, five
Money counts, no jive!

Verse
A dollar buys a red balloon
Or candy if you like.
But if you keep on saving,
You could buy a brand new bike!
Four quarters make a dollar bill,
One hundred pennies, too.
But, if you saved a million . . .
Just think what you could do!

Repeat Chorus

Now it's your time
To rap along with Mr. Dime.

Repeat Verse

Repeat Chorus

GLOSSARY

borrow (BAR-oh)—to take or receive something with the promise of returning it

dimes—coins worth 10¢ each

earned (ERND)—to be paid for work done

nickels (NIK-ulz)—coins worth 5¢ each

pennies (PEN-eez)—coins worth 1¢ each

quarters (KUORT-uhrz)—coins worth 25¢ each